Life Cycles

Wendy Conklin, M.A.

Consultant

Sterling Vamvas
Chemist, Orange County
Water District

Image Credits: p.17 (bottom right); blickwinkel/
Alamy; p.9 (top) Bruce Coleman Inc./Alamy; p.8 (top
right); E.R. Degginger/Alamy; p.21 (center) David
Barlow Photography; pp.7 (bottom left & top right),
8 (both bottom), 10–11, 13–19 (illustrations) Travis
Hanson; backcover, pp.4–5 (background), 7 (top left
& bottom right), 10–11 (top), 12–13 (background),
14–15 (background), 16 (bottom right), 17 (top),
18–19 (background), 20–21 (background & top), 22
(left), 24–27 (background), 27 (middle left & right),
31–32 iStock; p.13 (top right) Fred Bavendam/
Minden Pictures/Newscom; p.14 (top center); Suzi
Eszterhas/ Minden Pictures/Newscom; p.15 (bottom
right) Jim Zipp/Science Source; p.9 (bottom left)
Mark Smith/Science Source; p.10 (top left) Ted
Clutter/Science Source; p.18 Tom & Pat Leeson/
Science Source; pp.28–29 (illustrations) J.J. Rudisill;
all other images from Shutterstock.

Library of Congress Cataloging-in-Publication Data

Conklin, Wendy, author.
  Life cycles / Wendy Conklin; consultants, Sally Creel,
Ed.D., Curriculum Consultant, Leann Iacuone, M.A.T.,
NBCT, ATC, Riverside Unified School District, Jill Tobin,
California Teacher of the Year Semi-Finalist, Burbank
Unified School District.
    pages cm
  Summary: "Every day, living things grow and change.
How do they do it? Find out by exploring life cycles of
elephants, salamanders, humans, and more"—Provided
by publisher.
  Audience: K to grade 3.
  Includes index.
  ISBN 978-1-4807-4637-4 (pbk.)
  ISBN 1-4807-4637-1 (pbk.)
  ISBN 978-1-4807-5081-4 (ebook)
1. Life cycles (Biology)—Juvenile literature.
2. Mammals--Life cycles—Juvenile literature.
3. Animal life cycles—Juvenile literature. I. Title.
    QH501.C66 2015
    571.8—dc23
                              2014034228

Teacher Created Materials

5301 Oceanus Drive
Huntington Beach, CA 92649-1030
http://www.tcmpub.com
ISBN 978-1-4807-4637-4

Table of Contents

The Circle of Life

All living things pass through a life cycle. Trees, insects, animals, and even you grow and change. At first, all cycles may seem the same. Living things are born, they grow, reproduce, and die. But take a closer look, and you'll see that each kind of life cycle is a little different. Both butterflies and dogs have life cycles. But they are not the same. A butterfly begins life as an egg that hatches. A dog is born live from its mother. They grow up in different ways, too.

Throughout nature, the pattern repeats. Grow. Change. Thrive. Reproduce. These same events happen again and again. The end of the cycle leads back to the beginning. A new **generation** is created. This is the circle of life.

Cycles and Spans

A life cycle is a set of changes or stages. A life span is how long the animal or plant lives. The final stage for all life cycles is death.

A Cycle for Every Life

Some creatures must travel through just one or two short stages of life before becoming an adult. Others must transform several times. For every creature, the journey leads to a new generation. And the cycle begins again.

Mysterious Metamorphosis

What happens inside the cocoon? For hundreds of years, this was a mystery. Now, scientists know that caterpillars dissolve. Their muscles and bones break down into a kind of goo. Then, they build new bodies. The most amazing part? Scientists have proven that moths can remember things that happened when they were caterpillars—before they were goo!

silkworm cocoon

Cocoons come in all sorts of shapes, sizes, and colors. Some look like candies. Others look like twigs or leaves. Some even look like gold!

Moth Magic

As they grow, insects change form. Some think this change is magical. But it is a natural process called **metamorphosis**.

Many insects, like moths, have four stages in their life cycle. First, adult moths lay eggs on plants. An egg hatches, and a **larva** is born. A moth larva is called a *caterpillar*. A caterpillar eats everything it can. Then, it finds a safe place to hide—perhaps under a leaf. It wraps itself in a soft shell called a *cocoon*. This is the **pupa** stage for a moth. Inside the cocoon, a moth changes. A few weeks later, an adult moth breaks out of the cocoon. Once the adult lays eggs, the cycle will repeat.

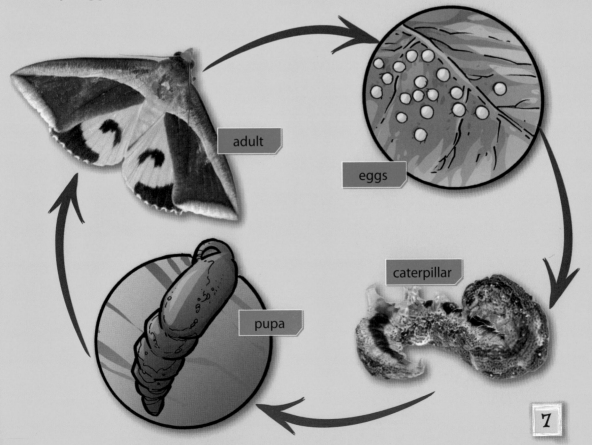

adult

eggs

caterpillar

pupa

Slippery Salamanders

Amphibians are animals that can live underwater and on land. Salamanders are a type of amphibian. Some live on land. And some live in water. Most salamanders lay eggs in water or on the wet ground. When the eggs hatch, the tadpole stage begins. These tadpoles look like tiny adults. They use their tails to help them swim. Their gills help them breathe underwater.

Salamanders that live on land go through complete metamorphosis. Their fins and gills disappear. They grow lungs and legs. But some salamanders are different. The ones known as *mud puppies* grow lungs. But they also keep their fins and gills so they can keep living in water. Their life cycles can span a few months or five years.

eggs

larva

adult

The Mexican axolotl's (ACK-suh-LAH-tuhlz) gills look like feathers floating around its head.

Another Amphibian

Caecilians (see-SIL-ee-uhns) are amphibians, too. Caecilians look like mini snakes. They have sharp teeth and a bony head that burrows in the ground. Some are small, but they can grow to five feet long!

Traveling Salmon

On the floor of a stream or a river, a salmon lays eggs in a nest. In early spring, alevins hatch from the eggs. Alevins are just one inch long. After about six weeks, they grow fins, teeth, and scales and leave the nest as fry. Some fry turn into parr and develop dark oval marks on their bodies to help camouflage them. Fry and parr leave freshwater for saltwater. They are now smolts and look like tiny salmon. The currents take smolts to the ocean. Once they arrive in saltwater, they become adults. Salmon stay in the ocean for one to seven years. Then, they swim back to where they were born to spawn.

A Sack Lunch

Eggs provide many animals with their first meals. They contain everything animals need to grow strong. Salmon fry eat what's left of their eggs before they swim to the ocean.

eggs

alevin

fry

spawner

smolt

adult

parr

Adult salmon travel thousands of miles to return to their nest and lay their eggs. They fight powerful currents and never even stop to eat!

Odd Octopuses

Octopuses begin as eggs. After a male octopus mates with a female, he dies. The female ties the eggs together and hangs them from her den. The female spends all her time guarding her eggs. When they finally hatch, she is so weak that she dies.

At first, baby octopuses are only as big as a grain of rice! These newborns are called *paralarvae*. They swim to the top of the ocean to find food. Whales and other fish eat many of them. After a few weeks, the paralarvae swim to the ocean floor. There, they grow fast. Predators eat many of them. Those who survive grow into adults. Adults lay eggs, and the cycle repeats.

Hide and Seek

Adult octopuses protect themselves by blending in. They use their muscles and skin to blend in with rocks. They also shoot dark ink to hide themselves.

A mother octopus's den is also called her *garden*.

eggs

paralarva

octopus

13

Eagles Take Flight

Baby eagles develop and grow inside eggs. The yolk in the egg provides food the baby needs. Once the food is gone, the eagle pecks its way out of the egg. An egg tooth on the tip of its beak helps it break open the egg. The **hatchling** depends on its parents for food. In just a few days, it becomes a nestling because it stays in the nest. At first, fluffy down feathers keep it warm, but real feathers grow within weeks. At two months old, it is called a *fledgling*. Soon after, this young bird becomes a **juvenile** eagle. The juvenile learns how to hunt from the adults. In about five years, it is an adult and is ready to mate.

hatchlings

nestling

egg

An eagle nestling can gain half a kilogram (one pound) of weight every week!

An eagle can live up to 30 years!

juvenile

adult

fledgling

A Partner for Life

Adult eagles find a mate and stay with that mate until death. Not all birds do this, but swans and turtledoves are a few that do.

Slithering Snakes

Most snakes begin their life cycle in eggs. After a few weeks, the snake uses its egg tooth to break out of the shell. The hatchling might not leave the egg right away. It can spend hours or days feeding off any leftover yolk. In no time, the hatchling grows into a juvenile snake. During this stage, it learns to hunt for food. As it grows, it molts, or sheds, its skin. Finally, the snake reaches the stage of an adult. Then, it is ready to lay eggs so the cycle can start again.

There are some snakes that give birth to live young. These include rattlesnakes, boa constrictors, and adder snakes. Other snakes carry their eggs inside their bodies. The babies hatch from the eggs inside the mother.

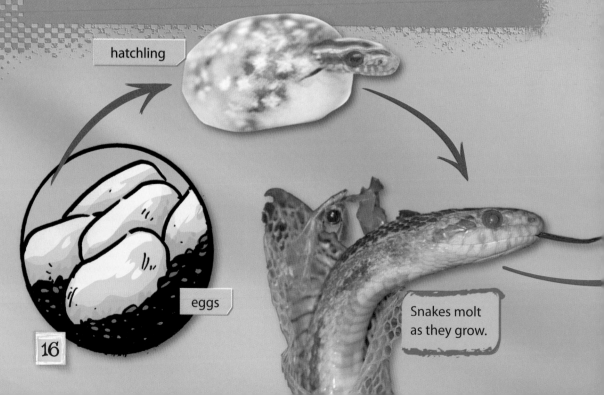

hatchling

eggs

Snakes molt as they grow.

Snakes continue to molt as they grow.

adult

juvenile

Moving Right Along

Once outside the shell, hatchlings are hungry. So they quickly slither away. If they hang around, another hatchling might eat them!

Snake eggs aren't hard like chicken eggs.

They are soft like leather!

17

Building a Beaver

What do beavers, elephants, and people have in common? They are all mammals! Mammals go through a life cycle, too. First, the egg stage happens inside the mother. Then, a live baby is born. For beavers, this happens in the spring. After birth, mammal life cycle stages can have different names. For example, baby beavers are called *kits*. At one year old, they are **yearlings**. They live with their parents and new kits in a lodge. They do this for safety. At two years old, beavers are juveniles. This is when they leave the beaver lodge and look for a mate. By winter, they are adults and start their own families. And the cycle starts again.

Mammals Make Milk

Mammals are known for the way females care for their young. Mothers feed their young fresh milk. Most mammals are also covered with hair. They can live in a wide variety of places.

Beavers build lodges with branches and mud. Some can only be entered by traveling underwater.

Yearlings help their parents with new kits. They gather food for them, help groom them, and spend time playing with them.

kit

yearling

adult

juvenile

19

Life as an Elephant

An elephant is another type of mammal. Its life cycle has three main stages. First, a mother carries a baby inside her. After 22 months, the calf is born. The mother teaches the baby how to live, eat, and clean up. By 10 years old, the calf is weaned. This means it no longer drinks its mother's milk. Then, it becomes an **adolescent** (ad-l-ES-uhnt) until age 17. The boys, known as *bulls*, hang out in groups. But the girls tend to stay close to their moms. By age 18, an elephant is an adult. Adults look for mates, and the cycle starts over. Elephants can live up to 70 years!

Baby Basics

An elephant only has about four babies in a lifetime. They can have twins, but that is very rare.

adult

adolescent

calf

unborn elephant

Inside the Womb

Young mammals develop inside their mother's womb (woom). When an embryo is first created, it can be hard to tell what kind of animal it is. Every animal starts out as a tiny blob! But after about four months, it becomes clear that this is a very small elephant.

Right before a baby is born, the mother elephant chooses an "aunt" to help care for the baby.

The Human Life Cycle

You, like every human, will grow in stages. For nine months, you grow inside your mother. Then, you are born. Childhood is the time from birth to adolescence. As an infant, you depend on your mother. You grow into a toddler and learned to walk. Then, you learn how to play. Your body is still growing. Your mind is growing, too. At 13 years old, you will be an adolescent, or a teen. Like an elephant, this is when you will become more independent from your parents. But most people live with their parents until they are at least 18.

Becoming an adult takes time. People don't wake up and realize they became adults overnight. Being an adult is more than how old you are. It's about making smart choices and taking care of yourself.

That is when you truly become an adult.

How to Live to 100

If you want to be a centenarian (sen-tn-AIR-ee-uhn), or someone who lives to a hundred or older, try these tips! They are all linked to living a long time.

✔ Eat healthy foods.
✔ Exercise daily.
✔ Brush your teeth twice a day.
✔ Spend time in nature.
✔ Get plenty of sleep.
✔ Laugh a lot.
✔ Be kind to yourself and others.

Growing Old

There is no age that is considered old by all people. If you are 9 years old, 70 years old may sound very old. But if you are 90 years old, 70 years old may seem young! People are finding ways to live longer and longer. And they are finding ways to be healthier and happier in old age.

From Seeds to Trees

Even plants have life cycles. For a tree, this begins at **germination**. This is when a seed begins to grow. A seed becomes a **seedling** when a root and stem grow from it. In time, the stem grows larger, leaves form, and it turns into a **sapling**, or a very young tree. Branches develop, and more leaves grow. This can take years, but finally the plant grows into a mature tree. Mature trees make seeds that drop to the ground. These form new trees.

A flower begins with germination, too. At this stage, a seed sprouts leaves. They are the first leaves that emerge from the soil. These leaves store food for the seedling. Then, a **bud** forms as a seedling grows. It opens slowly. Finally, the flower is mature and can make seeds for new flowering plants.

It's Cold in Here!

Seeds have special coats around them. The coat protects the seed from extreme temperature, injury, and bugs.

Don't Forget!

Animals such as squirrels help plant seeds. They gather and bury them. Later, they return to eat some of them. But some seeds get left behind or are forgotten. These forgotten seeds grow into new plants.

A Vital Connection

All living things grow and change. In time, they die. This is true for all creatures. But during those stages, life takes beautiful and surprising turns.

Young plants and animals are born every day. Some life cycles are short and dramatic. A fruit fly might live only 24 hours! Other life cycles are longer than we can possibly imagine. Some trees live thousands of years! But each cycle includes exactly the stages each creature needs to survive and thrive in this world.

How Long Do Animals Live?

15

woodpecker

20

10

owl

5

fox

25

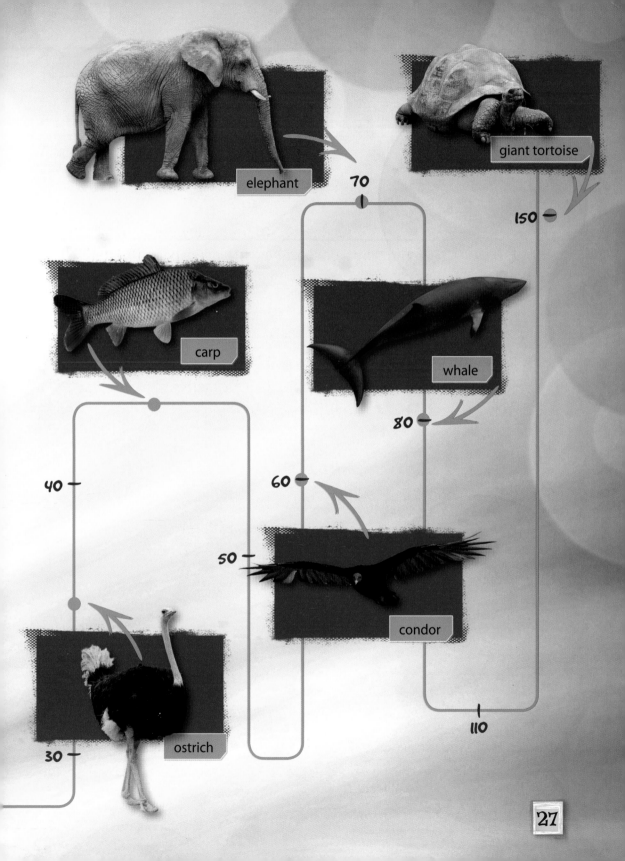

elephant

giant tortoise

70

150

carp

whale

80

60

40

50

condor

110

ostrich

30

Think Like a Scientist

How are insect and mammal life cycles similar? Experiment and find out!

What to Get

- coloring supplies
- hole punch
- index cards
- string

What to Do

1 Write the name and a short description for each stage of an insect's life cycle on index cards. Use one card for each stage. Draw a picture next to each stage.

2 Use the hole punch to make holes on both sides of each index card. Use string to tie the cards together in a circle.

3 Repeat steps one and two for a mammal's life cycle.

4 Compare and contrast the two life cycles. What stages in the life cycle are similar? What stages are different? Make a Venn diagram to show your observations.

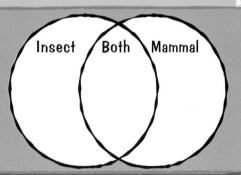

Glossary

adolescent—a young person or animal who is developing into an adult

bud—the part of a plant that grows into a flower, leaf, or branch

generation—a group of living things of the same species born and living during the same time

germination—the stage when a seed begins to grow

hatchling—an animal that just came out of an egg

juvenile—a young person or animal who is not yet an adult

larva—a very young insect that looks like a worm

metamorphosis—a major change in the form or structure of some animals or insects

pupa—an insect in the stage between larva and adult

sapling—a young tree

seedling—a young seed that has grown a root and a stem

yearlings—animals that are between one and two years old

Index

Your Turn!

Comparing Abilities

Make a list of things you could do as a baby.
Then, make a list of things you can do now.
Compare and contrast the two lists. What
things will you be able to do as an adolescent?
What will you be able to do as an adult?